T0198593

Prana

Thomas E. Berry, Ph. D.

PRANA

iUniverse books may be ordered through booksellers or by contacting:

iUniverse
1663 Liberty Drive
Bloomington, IN 47403
www.iuniverse.com
844-349-9409

Because of the dynamic nature of the Internet, any web addresses or links contained in this book may have changed since publication and may no longer be valid. The views expressed in this work are solely those of the author and do not necessarily reflect the views of the publisher, and the publisher hereby disclaims any responsibility for them.

Any people depicted in stock imagery provided by Getty Images are models, and such images are being used for illustrative purposes only.
Certain stock imagery © Getty Images.

ISBN: 978-1-6632-4587-8 (sc)
ISBN: 978-1-6632-4588-5 (e)

Library of Congress Control Number: 2022917696

Print information available on the last page.

iUniverse rev. date: 09/28/2022

Chapter 1

Driving through the wooded areas that lead to 'Prana', the Rocheau estate, not far from the great Merrimack River, the delivery truck's steward tried showing off to his girlfriend Sadie. Her small screams at turns through the tall pine trees made him laugh. Finally, to get his mind back on the road, she yelled, "What does "Prana" mean?"

Approaching the open stone entrance way to the great chateau of the Rocheau clan, the driver began slowing down. "Mrs. Rocheau says it's an ancient Hindu word for 'Paradise'. But I don't know, she's sort of a funny old thing. You'll see once we're there. I brought her son and his cousin Louis home yesterday. His Mother was very anxious to see them, which is normal for her. She is expecting her adopted daughter, Tres, home today. That will really make her happy."

Sadie became quiet as the Wallace Bakery truck pulled up to a patio at the back of the large brick office building behind the estate and by the swimming pool area. She was almost afraid to meet the hostess because of the various odd things said about her. Then the delivery boy added a couple of new remarks. "Yeah, she's French. You'll see. I've never met anyone like her. You'll see."

"Sacra Blue!" was distinctly echoed across a swimming pool and to the truck parked near by. "You're here already?"

1

"Yes, Mrs. Rocheau, Mr. Wallace thought you wanted them before your daughter comes."

"Well, yes, of course," a thin-bodied woman replied, crossing over by Sadie and continuing the conversation as if Sadie had the right to know. "My daughter has finally finished at Rosemont and is coming home. Since my son came home yesterday, with his cousin Louie. He's always fun. Oh, at last we'll be free to do what we want."

Sadie opened her mouth to speak, but was immediately cut off by the hostess. "Yes, and she's brining an old friend, Lili, home with her. I do hope I've thought of everything she asked to have ready for her. Those girls have been inseparable since childhood, although, I think Lili is a bit wilder than my darling Tres. For instance, she doesn't go to mass on Sundays. Imagine!"

Sadie was finally able to break into the hubbub, but not for long. "Does she…"

"Oh no, my dear. It's just…" Mrs. Rocheau suddenly stopped and called. "Did you bring the tarts I asked for?"

"Yes, Mrs. Rocheau."

"Oh, thank goodness. Tres loves them with coffee. She touched her head and said, "Oh, my, I did tell Manon to make fresh coffee, didn't I?" After a brief pause, the hostess answered her own question and continued. "Yes, I did."

The delivery boy came running up and handed Mrs. Rocheau a receipt, which she signed and thanked him. It was then that she noticed Sadie and waved as the young girl slipped into the truck for the return to town with her boyfriend. The hostess smiled as the vehicle left, but still had no idea of who was riding with her usual delivery boy. Finally, she thought, "Oh, it doesn't matter," and left the swimming pool area for the house.

Edith, the downstairs maid met the hostess in the entranceway. "James just called," she informed the surprised hostess. "Your daughter has just come through the front gate."

"Oh, wonderful," Mrs. Rocheau exclaimed and started toward the front door. It opened at that moment and Mother and daughter were soon in each other's arms with their joyous greetings. "Mon Tresor! And my Tres! At Last, at last," Mrs. Rocheau repeated over and over, repeating her nickname for her daughter.

After squirms and hugs were finished, Tres asked, "Is Henri home too?"

"Oh, yes," Mrs. Rocheau nodded as she said, "And he brought with him that cousin you liked so well at the last visit."

"Oh, Louie? I didn't care for him."

"Well, he certainly cared for you."

"Oh, don't be silly. He is Henri's friend."

"Whatever," the hostess exclaimed, "At least we are all home together and can do whatever we want to do."

At that moment a young man's scream was herd and a fast-moving young man was running down the wide, winding staircase, screaming, "Tres! Tres!" After a few calls, the brother had grabbed Tres away from the others and was walking her around the large entrance way.

While the others laughed and Mrs. Rocheau did a few steps backward, the group ceased its merriment and ended practically in a huddle in the middle of the large, orange hall. Everyone talked and enfolded someone in their arms. As the hubbub calmed down the hostess exclaimed, "I know you will all want to swim before dinner. So go put on your suits, splash a while and I'll have drinks brought to the garden patio and pool area."

Everyone agreed with glee and each ran off, chasing each other a bit and finally disappearing through the doors of the second floor. Some time later, the guests and friends slowly appeared by the swimming pool in their haberdashery apparel with their feet in the water as they waited for each other. Two maids brought out sandwiches and drinks, giving each seated swimmer a choice as they moved the tea caddies along the brick walk.

It was then that Mrs. Rocheau called Tres a side and said that she had something very important to talk with her about. Mother and daughter quickly slipped over into a rose trellis. Tres, to her surprise, finally noticed a very worried face on her mother. Her mother immediately explained her predicament. She had noticed something that was most alarming. Tres could not help but smile. Her mother was always taking things too seriously. Yet there was a bit of sarcasm in her vice that caused Tres to give her more attention.

"Darling girl, my Tres. Have you heard of any thing strange about your cousin Louie?"

"What do you mean mother?"

"Did he not make a great to-do over you when he visited last fall?"

"Yes, but it was only childish play. He's…"

"But what does he mean to Henri?"

"What do you mean? He's his cousin."

The Mother walked a few steps away from her daughter and then turned, "Oh, Tres, I saw something last night that has upset me terribly."

"What Mother?"

Mrs. Rocheau could not speak, but walked away again, folding her handkerchief and practically crying.

"Mother, darling. What is wrong?"

Holding back her tears, Mrs. Rocheau whispered, "I saw them on the bed doing things that men shouldn't do."

"What? Mother what are you talking about?"

"I can't say. I just don't believe it."

"What? Mother?"

After a pause, Mrs. Rocheau whispered, "Let's wait for your father. He is better at explaining things."

"When will Dad be home?"

"I'm not sure. He called from New York and said something about a conference. I hope it's not about some woman."

"Oh mother, Dad's true to you."

"That's another matter. This is far more serious."

"Tres could not help but laugh a small whimper."

"Is it funny?" The mother asked her daughter.

"No it isn't, but I don't know what it is. I've seen men pull their pants out of their derriere, but I never question it."

"Darling, it's not that. It's, well, you remember that our family goes all the way back to the Revolution. In those days of the old regime our estate was in the Providence of Berry, which is now part of Paris. Well, I remember that I was told that we had an uncle who was guillotined for some crime that Louis V did not approve of. It involved two men. We'll ask Father about it."

"Yes, let's do."

"He'll be home tomorrow. He'll know and explain."

"Probably does it himself," Tres teased.

"Heavens," Mrs. Rocheau exclaimed. "You don't know do you?"

"No, Mother, I don't know. I'm just talking."

"You go swim. I'd better check on the dinner."

As they parted her Mother said, "Now don't you worry about what I said."

"I won't, Mother. It is probably just a misunderstanding, anyway."

"Must you always tease me, my darling?"

"Oh, mother, I thought that was funny."

"Maybe it was, but we'll see what your father says when he comes home this evening."

"You plan to tell him?"

"Of course. It's too important to avoid. I want your Father's explanation."

Tres laughed as the two ladies went to their rooms overlooking the garden and pool.

Chapter 2

In the suite of Prince Benri de Rocheau.

After arriving home that evening, Prince Benri de Rocheau followed the instructions given to him by the maid from his wife and went immediately to his suite on the second floor. Once at the heavily inlaid gold of the doorway to his room, he stopped, straightened his coat and opened the large double door.

"Benri!" his wife greeted him from across the large heavily decorated bedroom, which was full of light from the large balcony windows dominating the center of the room. In seconds the wife was in the arms of her husband, talking very fast in French. The prince noticed Lili and his daughter in the room and stepped aside to greet them. Mrs. Rocheau took his arm again and began walking him around the two-canopied beds. It took a couple of minutes for the hostess to calm down before she allowed the others to speak.

The prince greeted his beautiful daughter Tres and her friend Lili, whom he always enjoyed having as a guest. The four friends and relatives finally agree to meet in the garden patio for drinks as soon as the Prince had given a maid his briefcase and instructions. The talking did not cease, but the group was finally seated in a teahouse beside the swimming pool.

Knowing that a family matter was to be discussed Lili excused herself, so she could make some phone calls. Because the Prince always loved teasing Lili, he told her not to be too long. She laughed and went into the library.

"Now as I understand it from what Mrs. Rocheau told me on the phone in New York yesterday, there has been sort of a misunderstanding or something between Henri and his cousin Louie?"

"Yes, Dad, but mother simply didn't understand what they were doing."

The Prince laughed and so did Tres.

"Naturally your mother would have it all mixed up. I don't know how many times I've explained the trouble with your great uncle during the reign of Louis V. She just refused to believe it. No wonder she's so afraid of something pertaining to Henri."

"But Dad, I hardly understand it myself. It's something sexual, but what could they be doing?"

"Now don't play coy with me Tres." You've studied history. In ancient days it was a common practice among men. Women were often degraded. No don't wince. It's true. Even in every war, men would do this sort of thing." The prince raised a hand, made a circle with his fingers and pushed a finger from his other hand into the hole.

Tres blushed, laughed then ran out of the room.

The prince grinned, stood up and went up the hall to his son's bedroom. When he opened the heavy, encrusted door, Henri yelled! "Dad!" Than he and Louie ran over to greet the Prince. The cousins have been friends for years. Even as boys they had been allowed to go on camping trips and hiking vistas. Because of their closeness and the length of their friendship, the Prince had never suspected that a deeper meaning was slowly developing in their hearts. The Prince saw them as just close friends, they saw themselves as buddies, companions and partners. Whatever physical habits had developed was their secret... discussed, practiced and taken for granted.

Yet, the Prince decided, it was perhaps time to step into the mirage. What might have been developing as real, could also just be an illusion, ripening slowly, unreal, but hallowed. He approached the subject via an example. During a card game, which the Prince liked playing with the boys, he suddenly mentioned an incident that he had heard about at a board meeting in the Morgan International Bank. It seems that an established financial expert had excused himself for a moment and went to an open window. Before his colleagies realized anything unusual, the man jumped out of the 90th floor building. "No!" was expressed by several members of the board.

The Prince looked at Louie and Henri and said, "Terrible things can happen when you go against social norms."

Louie and Henri looked at each other and Henri said, "Dad this is not us. We would never even considered such a fate." He explained that the feelings they had for each other were based on memories in the mountains at the Rocheau's summer cabin or in their boat on the near by lake. They had too much to live for to even allow such a horible future. Henri said immediately, "Dad, Louie and I are on safe and steady ground. We would never think of such things. Besides, we have our family honor to uphold. We've too much to live for."

"That's what I'm afraid of," the Prince said. "You see, I think you two are keeping something from me. You've already got a plan, haven't you."

Henri and Louie both laughed and admitted that they were thinking of going to the Alaskan fishing ports for the summer. They had friends who got them a job on a fishing boat. Yes, they'd fish, hunt, and then live as hermits up in the mouontains. It was just to be an experiment in living.

The Prince was shaking his head. "Well you beat me. I was afraid something like this was coming, but I obviously waited too long to say something."

"Aw Dad, let us have our time in the sun. You did. You went into the French Foreign Legion was stationed in the desert. Wow, that must have been quite a change of life style. 18th century French furniture in your bedroom and suddenly you're sleeping on a sand dune." They all laughed.

Then the Prince asked, "Have you told your Mother?"

"No, not yet."

"Well, you'd better let me help you with that. Now, I don't want any "*lovey dovey*" business discussed." Henri and Louie looked at each other with a strange grin. They were beginning to understand what the Prince was suggesting. Henri started shaking his head slowly as if to show that his father was wrong.

The Prince, however, continued to believe that he was correct and took on a tone of trying to help the young men. He then said, "We'll just approach the subject as if you boys wanted a summer job. Let her find out the depth of your relationship later. Remember, none of the love business between two men. She's not ready for that, even thought she had some ancient member of the family losing his head for loving some cousin."

Henri pretended to understand what his father was referring to and said, "We'll be careful, Dad."

The Prince thanked his son and changed the subject. "Louie."

The Prince smiled, "Louie, how would your folks take it?"

"Easily." Louie laughed. They'll be glad to have me away from the house. They can drink more."

Henri jumped in, "Yeah, it will allow that Father of yours to empty all the bottles."

"Is he still hitting the stuff that hard?" Asked the Prince.

"Oh yes, it's sad!"

The Prince stood up and announced, "Well, I'm sure I can fix up things here on the home front. You two go on with your plans. However, before you go, Henri, I want a word with you. Goodbye, Louie."

Louie left and Henri stayed behind. The Prince began talking immediately. "My son, you've got to keep something in mind. You are heir to this vast estate. Your Mother and adopted sister are in your keeping, as well. Now, are you sure you want to explore this emotional thing with your cousin? I'm not, but I want you to think about it. Remember, you will be Henri de Rocheau. Like it or not, you'll be quite a figurehead between the old regime and the people of this valley. It's something you should consider carefully."

"I shall, Dad, but let me have this summer. Please."

The Prince smiled. "I understand. OK. I will try and fix things with your Mother. I think I can. But the old girl has a mind of her own anymore. She's heard enough about the corruption of our present time. She thinks it's disgraceful, yet I've noticed that she sometimes quotes things she read or has heard, which makes me realize she's quite aware of certain things. Why the other day she referred to the Greek soldiers at Thermopolis as all being perverts. I almost fell out of my chair. But, when I asked her what that meant, she had a hard time figuring out what two soldiers could do to each other on a battlefield. I tell you, the Princess is not going to be easily pleased." He laughed.

"Oh, Dad, I doubt that Mother is going to see something wicked between Louie and me in her view of things."

"Why not?" the Prince asked. "She did see you two doing something in your bed."

"I told her the mattress was uneven?"

"And she accepted that explanation?"

"Oh Dad, of course. You know your wife. She'd accept any answer so long as it answered her question." He laughed and nodded his agreement.

Chapter 3

As soon as the Prince walked three rooms down the second floor hall, he opened the door of his daughter's room. "Dad," was heard as the heavily encrusted golden cupid decorations rang against each other on the wooden baseboard. Tres came running to her father who caught her in his arms and squeezed her tightly. "Ah, my pretty one." he whispered as he held her and swung her around the room.

After the joyous greeting, Father and daughter looked at each other and smiled. Even though she was adopted, it was a moment for enjoying the love that dwelled between them.

Mrs. Rocheau interrupted the loving harmony by saying, "Benri, you won't be so happy when you've heard the news." The father let his daughter down easily and asked, "What news?" Tres and Lili ran to the Prince and enveloped him in their arms as they both said, "We're going to have a baby!"

Only such news could have sprung the Prince into such fast action as he quickly said, "Who is having a baby?"

"Lili!" came floating through the air. Both young ladies had answered at the same time.

Yet it was Mrs. Rocheau's remark that commanded the scene. "Yes, Henri, Lili is going to have a baby."

"But why?" the Prince exclaimed, but then changed his tone. He looked at the girls and said, "You ladies promised that you would behave and now Lili's pregnant. By the way, Tres, you're not having a baby, are you?"

In an aggravated tone Tres answered, "No, Dad, I'm not, but I wish I were."

Her Mother jumped up and exclaimed. "Heavens, how ridiculous. One doesn't get a baby by chance! There has to be some sense of love and responsibility to it." With this statement she left the room.

The others laughed. "Oh, Mother," Tres continued. "Many of the ladies at Rosemount are pregnant."

The Prince's eyes widened and he angrily asked, "What the hell is going on up there? What are they teaching at that damn expensive school? It's disgraceful!"

Lili shook her head. "No Sir, it's the thing anymore. My generation believes one should live freely and also carry the burden of children."

"Well, I'll be damned! And what are we fathers supposed to do? Finance a drop-off clinic?" He then laughed and spoke more seriously. "My ladies, listen to me, I do not condemn you for such an attitude, it's your generation, as you say, but my generation doesn't agree. We still respect the family and I hope you will eventually do so yourselves. Tres, I'm so glad you're not pregnant. Lili will have a rough time bringing up a child. She has no idea the pressures she will go through. I hope she is ready."

"But Dad," Lili addressed the Prince, "I've called you Dad all my life and I know you'll help me."

"Well, I suppose so, but your generation seems to be too independent to ask for help. But, we will see."

At that moment the Princess returned and showed her displeasure in having their guest in a pregnant state and her daughter being encouraged to also have a baby. Once she fully understood, she turned on Lili and said, "Lili you've got your nerve. We've been like parents to you and you now act so irresponsible?"

The Prince interrupted and said, "Well, enough of this banter. Of course, we'll help Lili and we'll certainly hope that Tres will listen to us. No need to have a baby just because everyone is." He shook his head and laughed. "What a world it's become. It used to be disgraceful to have a baby out of wedlock, now it's the thing to do. I don't like it. There are too many babies out there abandoned and needing help."

Tres laughed too. "Oh Dad, you just want an old virgin around the house."

Her remark set up a new tone to the conversation. The Princess said she wanted to visit their relatives in Paris for their understanding of the present generation. Lili said that she was going home, but the Prince assured her that he would help her. Tres said she'd go with Lili to help calm the nerves of her friend's family. Everyone was now thinking of the new angel coming into their lives.

As the Prince started to leave, Henri entered the room. He stopped and asked Henri, "Have you made plans for the far north trip? Let's go to your room and you can explain." And they left together, talking down the hall.

"Yes, Dad. We're going to Maggiore for some shopping."

"But you spent a summer two years ago in the Alps. Why go there now to shop?"

"Dad, don't you remember that marvelous shopping area by Nukab? We'll stop in Milan. I want to get some recordings for our stay in Alaska."

"Good God, what a trip. Italy and then Alaska. Haven't you spent all the money Princess Cleric left you?

"No, she had that diamond collection, remember?"

"Well, carrying jewels is not wise these days."

"I won't Dad. I cashed them in. That's how I'm able to shop for everything I'll need."

The Prince coughed and said, "Yes, but you don't fool me. You're thinking of the brunette in that shop. You even took her dancing."

"Right, and I might again."

"Why don't you marry her?"

"What would our grand Potentate in Paris say if I married outside the family? No, Dad, I'll bring you back a Husky. You'll see."

"No, I don't need another dog." Exclaimed the Prince. Just go!" Then the Prince said, "But you could show Louie the De Vinci 'Last Supper' in that famous, museum down there!"

"Louie has been there before Dad."

The Prince chuckled, "He'd probably be asking who's sitting by Jesus at the table."

"Yeah, leave it to Louie."

The Prince grinned and said, "Isn't it supposed to be Christ's boy friend, the Apostle John setting next to him?"

"Now you're trying to tease me. I'm leaving." And he left.

The Prince called to his maid and asked her, "What would you do with a son who is acting a bit strange these days?"

"Nothing Sir," Was her response.

The Prince was quiet and finally said, "Thanks. Well, I guess I'll look at the poem Louie gave me." The Prince slowly read to himself the poem.

"I was a child, and he was a boy.
Our trouble was one and the same.
Sought the answer to the question "why"?
He followed his cross in vain.

Beauty and truth we cherished in life.
And together our friendship grew.
Companionship faded and turned in to love.
A love that is known by few.
All that we asked was to be left alone.
Our happiness was full and free.
But a meaning in life brings on envy and strife.
And society would not let us be.
Time has a way of healing a wound.
But our problem is still the same.
I seek the answer to the question "why"?
He follows his cross in vain."

Chapter 4

A week later Henri and Louie took a morning flight to Milan, and spent the afternoon shopping at the magnificent Gallerena Vittorio Emmanuelle that is next to the splendid Duomlo, the world's 3rd largest cathedral. The La Scala opera house is also close by. Then they lunched and had fun at the San Siro Race track.

Finally, they took a cab to the four star Palace Hotel near the Academy of Fine Arts. Their room had a balcony that overlooked the Como Lake district. They signed up for excursions in a program called Unpack Once, which arranged trips and most meals. They enjoyed the large open doorway out on the balcony. It was there they first felt as if they were doing something extraordinary.

Sitting on lounging beds around the wide balcony, Louie suddenly stood and walked over to the banister and started talking softly. "Oh glorious world enwrap me. Take me into thy arms and comfort me."

Henri stood up and listened to his cousin. A flashing star lit up a mountain peak. "Just think Louie, the great Carthaginian ruler Hannibal led an army with elephants through those mountains."

Louie said, "God, imagine riding an elephant up there."

Henri then added, "Well, remember it was also that famous Russian general that led a Russian army through those icy passes on his way to defeat the Italians for his beloved mistress."

"Who was that?"

"Catherine the Great."

After a slight pause, Louie asked, "Did she really sleep with a horse?"

"That's the legend." Henri replied.

Louie smiled and said, "I like talking about history with you."

"We'll have plenty of time for that in Alaska."

Louie laughed and slowly stepped into Henri's shadow. However, when he tried taking his cousin's hand, he was rejected. Both men stood facing each other, barely able to breathe, both pondering the moment and both moving toward it.

Henri, with no explanation, quickly turned and went to his bed, followed by Louie. The dream of Como's majesty had overcome them.

In a soft voice, Henri said, "Let's not go farther now." After another pause, he added, "Lets sleep it off."

"I can't. I close my eyes and see warriors and battles in the high mountains."

"You probably see naked warriors because I spoke of the famous naked Greek fighters in the Persian war."

"Why would I think of them?"

"Because they were naked."

"Well that's disgusting." My thoughts were not in the gutter, but you dragged them down into the muck."

"I just remind you of what you actually think of the most."

"That's not true."

"What's your favorite topic?"

"I guess, Pornography."

"I rest my case."

"What case?"

"That you prefer nakedness to classical beauty."

"But naked is more beautiful."

"Oh, go to sleep. You're not worth talking to this evening."

"I'm talking about beauty."

"So am I. So, good night."

(A sudden knock at their door)

Louie gets up and opens the screen door. Their two traveling friends, Clyde and Jeff, ran in and express their delight at tomorrow's departure for Alaska.

Hearing news about their trip to Alaska, Henri joins the group. They assure their friends that the Fishing Boat in Alaska has accepted them as workers. "Let the money roar in." Jeff says, and adds, "I know Louie that you've never worked on a fishing boat before."

"You're right. I'll have to learn fast."

"Stay with me and watch," Jeff says. "I'll teach you."

"Great!" Louie agreed and sang a short ditty about catching fish.

Henri said, "Fishing is the only sport Dad taught him."

"The Prince did that?"

"Yes, he taught me to play, football and Louie to fish."

"We'll all have something to brag about."

Clyde joined in with a crooked grin, "Well, come here Louie and tell me all about your father's help." He then reached out and grabbed Louie pulling him into his bed and under the covers."

Henri yelled, "Lights out!"

Chapter 5

Anchorage Alaska

After landing near the major fishing village in Southern Alaska, the four companions went to the main office of the fishing boat company.

Satisfied that they had all been accepted. They went to their lodgings and spent the night.

Louie who opened the door dressed in his rubber fishing attire and crowing like a banshee to awaken his comrades suddenly swept the morning air into their large bedroom.

Jeff jumped up and pulled Louie into the bathroom, where he shoved his victim under the shower, saying, "Don't ever awaken me like that again damn it."

Soon all four fishermen were walking on board their first fishing boat named the "Peacock", ready to be fishermen. Jeff led them into the hutch for a cup of coffee and their assignments.

After sailing off into the cold northern waters, the men sat together until they reached the first rounds of the fishing area. Leaving Louie inside, the three others went out on deck to help capture the swarming cod. About an hour later, Jeff yelled down to Louis who was stationed in the storage hold, to prepare for the first load of fish. He was going to open the door for the fish to slowly slide down the shoot into the hold.

Louie yelled back that he was ready, but little did he know. As the novice stood in the middle of the walled storage hold, a side door opened and over a ton of fish poured down the shoot into the hold. They came so fast, Louis was knocked off his feet and sitting in fish up to his neck. His yell for help brought down Jeff, who helped him stand-up, only to slip again, and slide under the fish. "Oh shit." Yelled Louie.

Jeff laughed as he helped his comrade get up again, saying, "Well you sure are an experienced fisherman, I see."

Louie didn't laugh. He was to busy just trying to stand and brush off the fish that were caught in his apron and flipping and flopping around him. After that inept display, Louie was then demoted to the hutch were he had some more coffee and was rescued from the fish hold.

During the afternoon, Louie tried again to serve in the hold, but each time a load was emptied into the large area, Louie would be knocked off his feet, pressed to the floor and fighting for his life among the squirming fish. He spent the last hours of his first day in the hutch as a coffee server.

Over a beer in the local bar, the chief of the fishing boat stopped by the young men's table and suggested that perhaps Louie should not try working in the hold the next day. He could use him in the hutch. Every one agree, especially Louie. Of course, his pay would be reduced.

Back in their lodging that evening, after eating a supper guaranteed to add weight. Louie confessed that he never wanted to see another fish in his life, except of course on his dinner plate. The men laughed.

However, Henri knew that he had to make a choice. Either he abandon Louie to work in the city of Anchorage or quit being a fisherman himself. Later talking with Louie, he realized that his companion wanted to leave the "dirty, slimy" fish world and do something else. So, the two men left their comrades and went looking for employment in another line of work. Henri was sorry because he had made a considerable amount of money that day, but he knew he had to go with Louie because their togetherness was the cause of their trip. That was clear and they parted from their friends.

Once alone, Louie thanked Henri for his sacrifice. He also reminded Henri of their two friends in California, Jean and Jim. They had an antique business that was quite successful. "See," Louie would often say in his rebuttal to Henri's analysis of their situation, "They are very happy together and quite successful."

"I'll never forget the dinner they had for us once. They had decorated the table with fine things from their shop. When I sat down I noticed that my utensils by my plate had Fragonard's beautiful pictures in graved in the fine silver. They thought the design reflected my personality. How we laughed."

Henri would comment. "Surely you don't want us to go into the antique business?"

Louie spoke up. "I'll bet we know more about the old stuff than they do. After all, we grew up in palaces of the old régime. We're stuffed full of the price of things. Take a gorgeous commode. Would either Jeff or Clyde know that it's 18ᵗʰ or 15ᵗʰ century? Hell no, they wouldn't. They wouldn't even know what the ormolu's represented."

"I think you're wrong. Besides, I do not want to be in the antique business. I want us to find something else."

Henri concluded his view by saying, "Seems to me we did not think our plan though very well. We were planning to spend our lives together as fishermen and that didn't work out right."

"Your right about that. I never want to see another fish, unless it's grilled and ready to eat."

Henri laughed and then asked a very important question. "Well, what are we going to do?"

After a short pause, Louie said. "We'll first talk with Clyde and Jeff about our change and see what they'll suggest. After all, they know Alaska and we don't. We can also go to town here and see what is offered. We need to find something that interest both of us, especially, if we are really going to spend our lives doing it."

Henri commented. "Yes, for a lifetime, it had better be very worth while and good."

Louie laughed.

When their companions came from the trailer they were staying in, the four of them discussed the situation together. Several professions were mentioned, but Clyde and Jeff both thought that being woodsmen would be quite practical. They explained, "You'd be in a wonderful area where no one would be disturbing you. You'd have your own life and could do whatever you really wanted."

Henri asked, "If it's so great, why did you leave it? After all, you did spend at least two years up in that wilderness."

Jeff spoke up, "Yes, we did and I look back at it as the happiest time of our lives."

"Why?"

"You want to know why we left something we loved, right?"

"Yes.

"Well you'd have to live that life to answer that question. You'll see what we mean if you try it."

Louie began singing a funny woodsman's ditty.

Henri looked at Louie and said, "Let's try it."

Chapter 6

Fortunately for Henri and Louie their comrades had lived in a cabin in the mountains in the past and could give them plenty of information about what they should have and where the best areas living and hunting were located.

After shopping in a couple of the camping stores in Anchorage. The four friends broke up as Jeff and Clyde had to go to their positions on the fishing boat named "Peacock". The group said their goodbyes and parted. Jeff and Clyde went to their work full of doubt about the possibility of their friends being woodsmen in the rugged country area they knew.

The Henri and Louie were full of enthusiasm and continued shopping. All went well until they came to the list of hunting stores their friends had made for them. They entered and were big eyed as they looked at the countless areas of guns, large, small, well known and the never heard-of-types. Louie picked out a beautiful 12-gauge shotgun with a fancy white leather carrying case, while Henri listened to the salesman's recommendations. He finally chose the gun most highly recommended by the clerk— a scoped 30/30 rifle for big game and protection.

They decided it was time for lunch after the drooling over the gun selection. Greatly satisfied, they went to a local bar and had the rib special. Stuffed, they took the easy walk over to a well-known real estate office and were soon looking at available cabins in their picture books. Again they were filled with rapture for some of the available properties were for rent and came furnished and had all the modern conveniences. They could move right in without much effort. The chosen cabin was on the edge of a divide in a hill and the views from the balconies were simply unreal because of their formations and depths. No doubt about it, they had been lucky again and made arrangements to have their boxes shipped down from the boat warehouse in Anchorage. Since it was soon to be dark when they finished. They rode with the salesman back to the port and completed the sale. Then they rode with the movers back to the newly rented deluxe cabin as night settled in. They had been lucky to do so much in one day.

Henri had to make the fire in the large fireplace, as Louie confessed that he had never made a fire in the fireplace at home. His excuse made sense. "You know how large our living room is back home. A servant always made the fire, so don't expect me to do it without practice."

Henri soon became used to hearing Louie's complaints and finally just up and did most of the household chores rather than argue over the details. He was terribly fond of Louie and had willingly fallen into the tricks Louie pulled in order to get Henri's approval for their adventure. However, even paradise can have its limits. The limits came the first evening at their lodge.

Having done most of the moving and arranging of their things, Henri suggested they go to bed after they finished the deli food they had brought with them.

"No. I don't want the deli stuff." Louie said, "Let's cook that steak for our first dinner."

"Naugh, I'm not that hungry and that would take too long."

Louie said. "You probably want to go straight to bed, right sleepy head?"

"You're right. I'm dead tired and couldn't play Romeo without falling off the banister."

"I guess I'll go to bed as well. After all, it is our first night in our new home. We should celebrate."

"Listen, Louie, I know what you've got in mind and I don't feel like it. I feel every muscle crying out for help. I feel like I lifted the Grand Canyon to day."

"Well, you weren't the only one lifting. I did my share."

Henri looked around and said, "You sure did. That little bouquet on the recorder sure looks heavy."

"Smart Ass!" Louie shouted, grabbed his pajamas and walked into the bedroom. Then he slammed the door.

Henri ate some of the deli food, read the local paper and played a recording he liked. After a while Louie came out and said, "I'm all showered up. Surely you're not as tired a you were."

"How's the shower?"

"You'll have to fix it, I'm afraid."

"What's wrong?"

"You'll find out."

"Oh, well I'll fix it in the morning."

"Why not now?"

Henri stood up and said, "Listen, princess. One more line about that shower and you'll get another one." Then he took his paper and went to the corner chair in the bedroom, where he could read with a flashlight until the first time Louie started snoring, and it didn't take him long. Henri put the paper down and lay there wondering.

Chapter 7

Louie's screams of joy and delight awakened Henri and caused him to leap from his bed and hasten into the large living room. The light from the windows was so bright he was practically blinded by the bright snow that reflected through the large glass windows.

Louie saw him coming and yelled most happily, "It snowed."

"That's Alaska for you," Henri shuddered and sat down across from the ashes in the fireplace.

"Isn't it magnificent?" Louie practically barked.

"Guess you think we need a dog."

"Why not? Think at how playful he would be in that gleaming whiteness."

"Better still, let's let you clean the side walks while I try making some breakfast."

"Are you going to continue being an ass this morning?"

"You're the ass. What have you done but complain ever since we came here?"

"That's not true. I have merely tried to make it the home we talked about back home. We were going to be so satisfied with a place of our own, where no one would be around to accuse us of anything."

"Don't you see that we've got to prepare this place for decent living? It's a mess now and I won't live that way."

"Neither will I."

"Well, act like it. You're just too used to having servants. I will not be your slave. You've got to help me and be a part of the solution."

"Please don't pick on me! It's not the way you talked about our palace in the far north when we were planning to come here."

"True, but how was I to know you were so inexperienced with life's rudimental necessities?"

"Were you expecting Paul Bunyan? You knew how spoiled I was in that drunken home I had."

"I think now I was merely trying to save you from it."

"Then please save me Henri." Louie said with a trembling voice.

Henri then reached out and enfolded Louie into a blanket and rolled him onto the couch with him.

"Thanks Henri! I needed that."

Chapter 8

Snow scrapping the sidewalk awakened Henri and he hurried to the large wooden door. When he finally pulled it away from the snow that was stuck to it. He heard the rough voice of Clyde. Their friends had come and cleaned their walk as a welcoming-home present. Louie called them in and the four companions settled into the kitchen, where Henri finally had a roaring fire in the large wood-burning stove.

"Wow, I sure didn't mean to break up your sleeping late this morning," Jeff said and laughed.

Louie remarked, "Jeff, if you're going to start teasing me already, I'll throw you into that snow pile out there."

They all laughed.

Jeff commented, "Honey Bunch, when you can throw me into that snow pile, I'll let you do it."

Louie replied, "You just want to get me into the snow."

Jeff rebuttals, "Well, one never knows." Then he laughs, too.

Henri turned the conversation to their newly purchased outdoor hunting gear. And asked, which clothes would be best for a hike out in that snow?"

Clyde pointing to the white leather pullover caps with ear coverings and quickly answered, "Oh, never take a cap like that into such a snow.

This snow has produced a deep early spring ground cover. You'd never hear a bear coming up to you in this stuff."

"Really?" Henri responded.

"Gosh, Louie added, "We've got to be very careful."

"You betcha" Clyde injected. "I'd say that it might be wise for us to go with you on your first expedition."

"Yes," cried Louie and they all agreed. Once suited up with their guns hung over their shoulders, they marched out into the snow.

At the end of the driveway they waited for Louie, who was closing the door. Clyde yelled, "Make it tight. Bears can open it."

Louie said he did as he turned to join them. He took a step and lost his balance. Hands flying, he scooted, and slipped all the way down to the truck.

"Don't bust'em." Jeff teased.

Louie stuck out his tongue, saying. "You'll be sorry if I do."

At the truck they all put on their snowshoes for the long walk in deep snow.

Chapter 9

As the men started off on their hike, Jeff teased Louie. "Oh, look, Louie's got a white leather sheath for his shotgun."

"So you did buy it," Clyde commented.

Louie answered, "Yeah, I'd never seen a white case before."

Jeff flipped his wrist and said, "Oh, that's the prettiest thing I ever saw."

Clyde growled at his partner. "No more teasing please!"

After moving quietly for a while, the huntsmen soon came upon bear tracks that were winding in and out through an area of small bushes and trees. Clyde spoke in a lower tone than he was usually speaking. "Hey, listen. I've seen this sort of underbrush before and it was just the sort of thing that bears like. They like to rub things off their fur when they go through the bushes."

Louie asked, "Then they could still be near here. Is that what you mean?"

Clyde nodded and looked at the others, then said in his low voice, "Let's keep our eyes and ears open. If you see a bear don't move suddenly."

Slowly the four walked into the green area they had been watching. Jeff in the lead jumped and suddenly said out loud, "Oh. Shit, watch out for the bear piles!"

Louie giggled a bit and asked, "Did you step in some?"

Clyde answered, "Yes, and they don't leave wipes!"

Jeff jumped in and said, "Let Louie show you how he cleans it."

"I've had enough of you," Louie called to Jeff.

He answered, "I'll say you have."

Louie said with acid in his voice, "Shut up, you bastard."

Henri joined them. "Well, if there were any bears near by, they will have run off with you guys yapping like that."

Clyde jumped in and said, "Didn't I tell you two to be quiet? Now let's try again." The huntsmen continued quietly.

After several miles, the bear tracks soon disappeared and the group entered an area filled with tall trees. They could see a large rocky area ahead of them. Louie suggested that they make a fire and have coffee. Clyde said they could not take the time because he and Jeff had to report to the fishing boat that evening.

Since they had stopped, they took time to have a leak on a tall tree. Marching again they passed several places where they had already been. When they reached the green area where they had seen bear tracks, Louie cried out, "Damn, I've lost my rifle."

Each huntsman had a question in trying to help Louie. "Where did you have it last?"

"I'm not sure."

"What about that rocky area? Did you put it down on the rocks?"

I don't think so. Sure don't remember doing that."

"Was it loaded?"

"I think so."

"What do you remember last about it?"

"We were here and I put it down so that I could use snow to wipe off the bear poop."

Jeff laughed, but Clyde gave him a look to shut him up!

"It's probably down in the snow." Henri suggested.

"Let's look around here."

For some time the men searched through the snow in the underbrush area, but they never came upon the white shotgun case.

Henri finally remarked, "We'll come back here tomorrow and look some more. Our friends have a ship to catch."

Louie started sniffing and finally producing tears.

Henri. Aggravated, told him, "None of hat. We'll find it tomorrow."

The huntsmen went back to the cabin and waved goodbye to their comrades, thanking them for the visit and asking them to repeat it.

Chapter 10

Entering their snowbound cabin, the hunters found a letter stuck in their front door. It seemed quite remarkable that a letter would be delivered in such weather, but when they opened it, they were confronted with another great surprise. It was a letter from Tres! A letter from home!

Before even starting a fire, Henri sat down in front of the fireplace, quickly joined by Louie. It was news from home and they both had long been longing for news from home. Trying to see the letter in Henri's hand, Louie gave up and said, "Read it aloud, please."

"Dear Henri,

Where are my mysterious and adventurous darlings hiding out? I hope you are either wading through snowdrifts or sitting by a wondrously flaming fire. Yes, happy and content! I'll bet you are wondering how I found you. Well, your friends, Clyde and Jeff, wired me your new address as they had promised. You see I do care about what was happening with you.

Our news is your news, too. Lili had a baby boy and she named him Shay! Doesn't he sound like the leader of our tribe?

I like to think so. With you not wanting to be our Prince, we'll have to wait for him to grow up, but time does fly by, as you know.

Your mother has Shay wrapped up in a beautiful silk Japanese cover. He is so sweet. I think he'll make you a fine huntsman. We intend to enroll him in Sunnydale, where you and I languish at that age. I think he'll take your place as ruler of the, shall we say mountain? Whatever, I hope he is happier and more content than you ever were.

Tell Louie that his parents are in Florida for their winter season and that they were glad to know where you are- (I told them). They'll be glad to hear from Louie, I'm sure."

Louie broke in. "Like heck they will. Down there you can't get Dad away from his bottle and mother from a bridge table. I know them too well and that does not include any worry about me."

Henri dropped his hand holding the letter, looked at Louie saying, "It would be fun to see them."

"Well let's go then," Louie said, astonished that he had said that.

Chapter 11

Henri criticized his mate: "Really? Just like that. You'd run off and leave the fortune we've invested here. You're expecting some relative to pay for us while leaving a tip."

"Don't be so sarcastic. I just want to go home."

"Well, we can't just walk off and leave every thing, besides, what about our arrangement? We were going to live forever and be so happy we wouldn't care what others think. Where are all those brave words now?"

"We don't have to part. I've held up my part of the bargain."

"Yeah, well what about Jeff? I'm not blind."

"Oh, that was nothing. He just likes to tease me."

"Some tease, I'd say."

"What are you trying to say? You want to split up?"

"I want you to start making sense. How can we split up, as you put it? We've taken it a little too far for that. You want to make fools of us? You'd better have a drink and think of what you're suggesting."

After a short pause, Louie apologized. "You're right. With you I'd found everything I always wanted, even though you are the highest rank in our clan. I was so proud of that. I was so proud that I had conquered the head of the Rocheau family for my longed for adventure."

"You dislike our family that much?"

"Yes, I'm sick of playing an 18th century clown."

Thomas E. Berry, Ph. D.

"You ignorant little pup. You're the clown only because you enjoy it. You certainly do not deserve to be a member of such a famous and legendary family. I'm ashamed of listening to you and getting involved in a pointless tirade."

"Don't try to kid me. You enjoyed our being together. Besides, there's enough room in our fickle family to allow anything we want. You enjoyed yourself with me and I know it."

"We went too far! Then I was curious, then amused. Finally I realized that I was enjoying something I had always avoided, even though it was in the family. I surrendered."

Chapter 12

"To save our souls," Louie said, "I suggest we go home and have a conference with the Prince and let him help us settle our affair. He's wise and saw a lot in the last war. He would understand our predicament and we can be open with him."

Henri looked at Louie and after a pause said, "Louie, I think that's the wisest thing you ever said. I agree and I'm proud of you."

A week of packing, selling and hiking in the snow passed quickly and the young men were sooner than expected siting on a cross-country train eastward. They wanted to fly, but they had so much to take with them, a train was the only practical vehicle. They rented space on a freighter and bought a cabin for themselves. The big cities quickly passed by: Salt Lake, Denver, Chicago and their transfer to an Amtrak train to Boston. They were picked up at the train station by a Rocheau Chauffeur and taken to the Rocheau estate. They arrived late in the night and went straight to their room. Word went quickly through the mansion that the young men had returned. Maids and cleaning ladies jumped into their positions and the grand palace was soon in full swing of the household routine.

Tres could not wait and early the next morning went into the men's wing of the large structure and turned on a light, awakening both cousins. "Tres!!" Was called by Henri and Louie at the same time. She hugged them both and said she'd have coffee brought up immediately.

Tying to leave for the coffee, Tres was caught by Henri who pulled her down on his bed and gave her a quick kiss.

Tres Jumped up and cried out, "Henri, Really!" He laughed and let her run to the door.

Louie, having watched the spectacle between his relatives, said, "Well, I guess I know who won the love battle!"

Henri quickly replied. "Don't be so sure you did. Tres and I have been in love ever since the second grade. She's used to my kisses. That doesn't mean she wants me. She is my adopted sister after all."

Louie whispered loudly, "Yeah!" Louie rebutted, "but I didn't travel across this blessed country to be a ring bearer for you."

Henri laughed and said, "It's the game we have to play. We love each other, but we both have our own feelings about each other."

Louie snarled, "You should work in a carnival."

When Henri went into the bathroom, Louie yelled, "I have as much of a right as you do?

"Yeah, if you shake the family tree a bit."

"Ha, Ha, Ha, wasn't that funny."

"Louie, your branch of the family is so far out in the tree, a squirrel would go crazy looking for it."

Louie protested. "Wait 'till the Prince comes. He'll say I'm correct."

"Let's hope for your sake."

"Did I hear my name mentioned?" The Prince said as he walked into the young men's room. He welcomed the boys, saying, "Well, so the wild west is not a life of comfort, n'est-pas?"

Louie quickly jumped from his bed and bowed to his great, great uncle. Trying to say every thing at once, he blurted out incongruous items about fishing boats and snowfalls. The Prince was highly amused.

Henri came out of the bath still drying himself. After greeting the prince, he laughed and said that the Alaskan wild had taught them a lesson, especially Louie.

The Prince sat down, took out a cigar and laughed, saying, "Well you stayed longer than I expected. What finally brought you back, a snowfall?

Henri commented, "You might say that. Seems that a touch of snow ate a very expensive white leather shotgun case and gun."

Louie barked, "Let me tell it, please. It wasn't my fault. We were attacked by a wild bear and I mislaid my gun."

Henri started laughing.

"Did the bear find it first?" the Prince asked.

Henri laughed harder holding his sides.

"That's not fair." Louie commented. "It was a serious error and we never could find my wonderful weapon."

"Shoot many bears with it?" The prince asked with a grin on his face.

Henri doubled over with laughter.

"Why must everyone tease me?" Louie asked, "Even you," he added pointed at the Prince. The Prince waved a hand for Louie to be quiet. "Listen my young Princesses, you two characters have returned at a most auspicious time. I'll remind you a bit of your own history and maybe you'll understand, Sit down and listen."

Chapter 13

"Let's go back to the glorious year, 1789. Yes, the year you two would have inherited an easy life on one of the Rocheau estates. Then those blasted peasants started their Revolution and left you out in the cold. Well, it seems that the Rocheau came out of the fray quite well off. You were spared your life of drudgery working."

"Yes, when they cut up la Belle France, the Ancient Regime was banished, but our branch of the family was not guillotined. It was just swallowed by Paris and the Rocheau became a Consulate. Well, that at least saved your necks."

"Now the good news is that the one great day given the old aristocracy is also our Fourteenth of February, Bastille Day. We can do any thing we like, drink, dance, sing, or even act crazy."

"So, you've come home just when your famous Auntie does her yearly visit. The La Belle Grande Princess will join the family at dinner with some remarkable news. It's always our most glorious and most majestic event."

Henri asked, "Why should that make us so happy?"

The Prince quickly said, "My how quickly the young forget the past." Continuing, he said, "Don't you remember, it was her family that persuaded Louie V to bring Marie Antoinette to France? Yes, it's true. Besides La Belle became the greatest party giver of the age back then.

Even when she comes here she puts on a lot of airs. You'll love talking to her, because her family had the Princeling who liked men and made quite a scandal of it. Louie V even had him guillotined. She'll tell you all about it."

"Well uncle, you seem' to be talking quite easily about it too. Does this mean that you now understand our situation?"

"Sure I understand. It must be in our blood, but it still doesn't make sense. What man would want to stick his ding dong into that hole, when a woman's got something warm for him." The Prince laughed.

Henri remarked, "Dad, it's more complicated than that."

"Oh, here we go, a man talking about love with another man."

Louie remarked, "But it can happen. I know."

The Prince laughed and said, "A butterfly like you. I'll tell La Belle about you two. She'll straighten you out." He laughed and left. Then he laughed again at the door.

La Belle went to Henri's rooms as soon as the Prince told her about Henri's situation. When she entered in all of her laces, pearls and jewels, Henri called out, "My Princess is here and ran to her He put his arms around her waist and did one circle knocking her almost off her feet. Knowing she doesn't care to dance, because it messes up her blouse, he stopped, but they hung on to each other. After a few flattering comments from them both, Henri walked her to the lounge and they sat down.

La Belle immediately exclaimed, "My dear, I know all about your problem. The prince has confided that you greatly need my advice. So, let's begin. Henri, first of all, I can't believe you'd hitched up with that brat, Louie, especially with Tres waiting for you. Henri shook his head as if the information couldn't be true. "Oh, but it is true. Now you must confess. You're surely not taken by the looks of Louie, right?

Well, maybe he can be a little diverting," La Belle said and then added, "but so can a sore toe."

Henri spoke up, "But La Belle, Tres is my adopted sister she doesn't want me?"

La Belle rebutted, "How little you know, how little you understand."

Henri asked, "You really think so?

"I know so!" She replied.

La Belle was adamant. "Am I not a woman?"

"Yes, and what a woman!"

"Thank you, but have you forgotten that you're a man and in position to become the head of a famous clan?"

"Of course, and I do love Tres. I have all my life. And I protected her. Yes, I did. Even when she wanted to play doctor when we were little. I never took advantage of her naivety."

La Belle continued her intervention, "But don't you realize that your action shows how much you loved and respected her even when you were children."

"Yes, it did and I love her still."

"Don't you realize that the family has always expected you to marry her? When your cousin Peirre's family was killed in that car accident, and Tres was the only survivor. Your family quickly took her in and adopted her. That way the Prince and Princess will be of the same proper family."

"Even if you have that odd streak in you that makes you want to play around with men, it's still no reason not to marry her. My husband could hardly pass a telephone pole with out thinking of a man's you know what."

"But I wouldn't want to embarrass her."

"Oh, she'd think it funny, not silly. She might have a thing for some woman's lipstick. Who knows?"

"What I'm trying to say is that men loving men is in nature and certain civilizations accept and some don't. At the present, most of the world is too stupid to catch on. Americans only think of balls. When they write up the history of our culture, they'll say that we only thought of baseball, football, basketball and bedrooms."

"You've got to be intelligent about the way things are in society and our culture. While it's true that you could point out many men of that sort in history, you must also remember that the mood changes with every historical period. Men do have a freer society today than at the turn of the century. There are men with men in every level of society today. So, it is up to you to choose your future I do not see you, two boys together. But, it's for you to decide."

"Now, having said all of that, I shall give you some good news."

"Our beautiful Treas is your adopted sister and Louie is your cousin. It would be wonderful to keep the marriage in our family. You now have the terrible duty to preserve our family name. Which do you choose as the next Princess dela Rocheau? Tres or Louie?"

"Yes, it can be a man such as Louie! You see, there is a long-kept secret among the family that explains how that can be. If in the final stage, should the choice be for either a woman or a man to be the Princess, the Rocheau family, so burdened with the fickle curse, will allow a male Princess to be the Princess just to keep it in the family. That's pride for you."

"Now, which Princess do you choose?"

Printed in the United States
by Baker & Taylor Publisher Services